With

to
Richard P. Gross

Reinforced binding suitable for library use.

Copyright © 1987 by Ruth Heller. All rights reserved. Published by Grosset & Dunlap, Inc., a member of The Putnam Publishing Group, New York. Published simultaneously in Canada. Printed in Singapore. Library of Congress Catalog Card Number: 87-80254 ISBN: 0-448-19211-X
E F G H I J
Jacket copyright © 1987 by Ruth Heller

# A Cache of Jewels

## and Other Collective Nouns

Written and illustrated by
RUTH HELLER

GROSSET & DUNLAP, NEW YORK

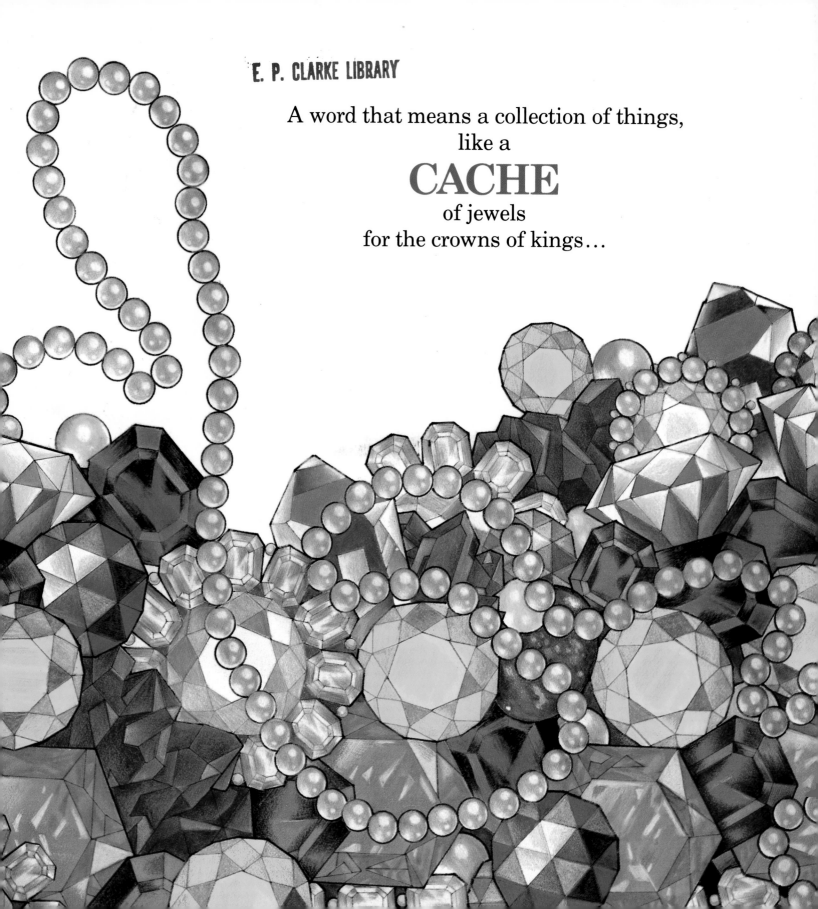

A word that means a collection of things,
like a

# CACHE

of jewels
for the crowns of kings…

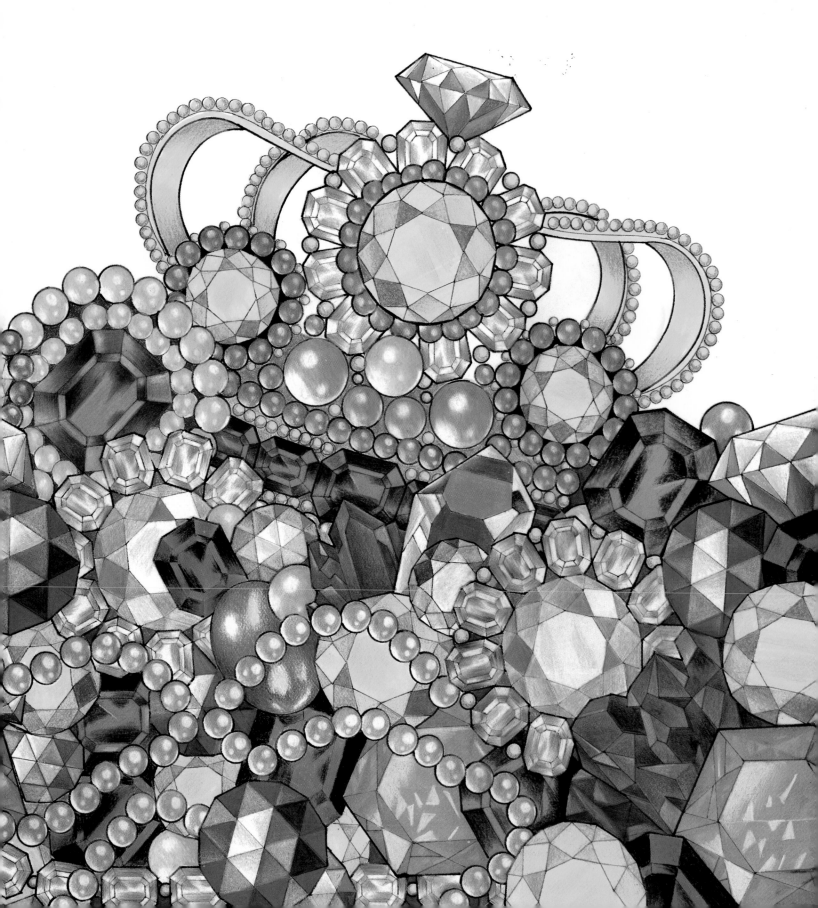

or a **BATCH** of bread all warm and brown,

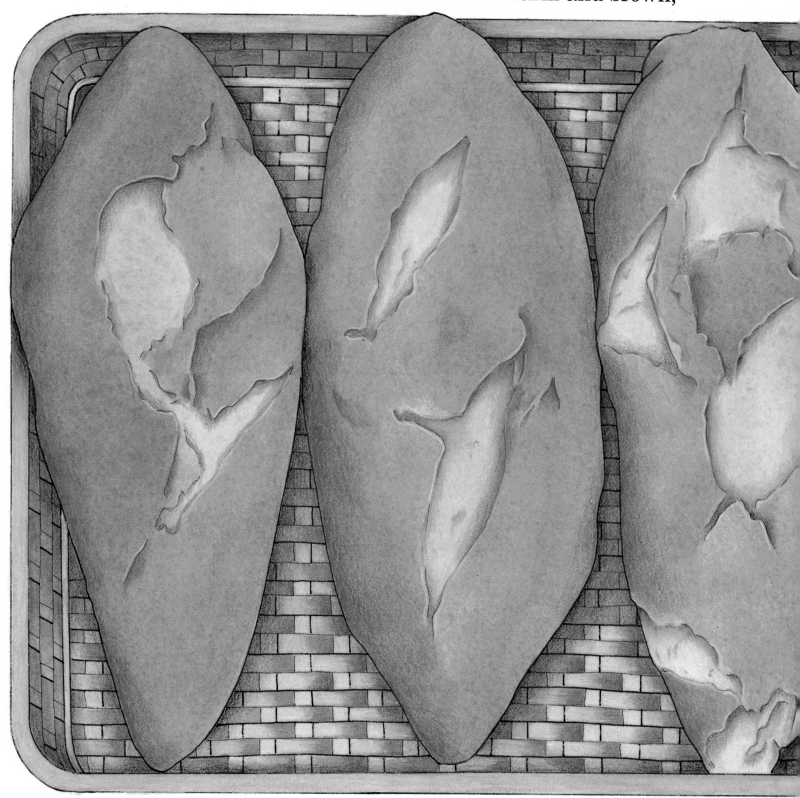

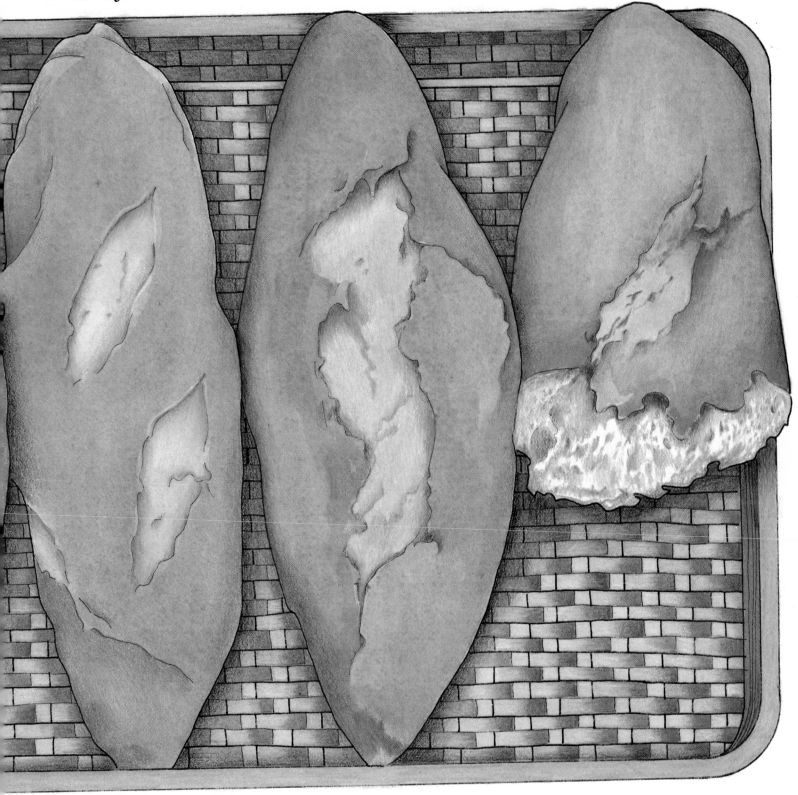

a **SCHOOL** of fish

a GAM of whales

a **FLEET** of ships
with
purple sails

a BUNCH of bananas

a
**CLUSTER**
of
grapes

a
**BEVY**
of
beauties
.

all different
shapes

a **MUSTER** of peacocks

a
**FLOCK**
of
sheep

a
**HOST**
of
angels
fast
asleep

a **BOUQUET**
of flowers

a
**SWARM**
of
bees

a **KINDLE** of kittens
a **POD** of peas

a **PARCEL** of penguins

a **FOREST** of trees

a
**COVEN**
of
witches
as
scary
as
these

a **DRIFT** of swans

a **CLUMP**
of reeds

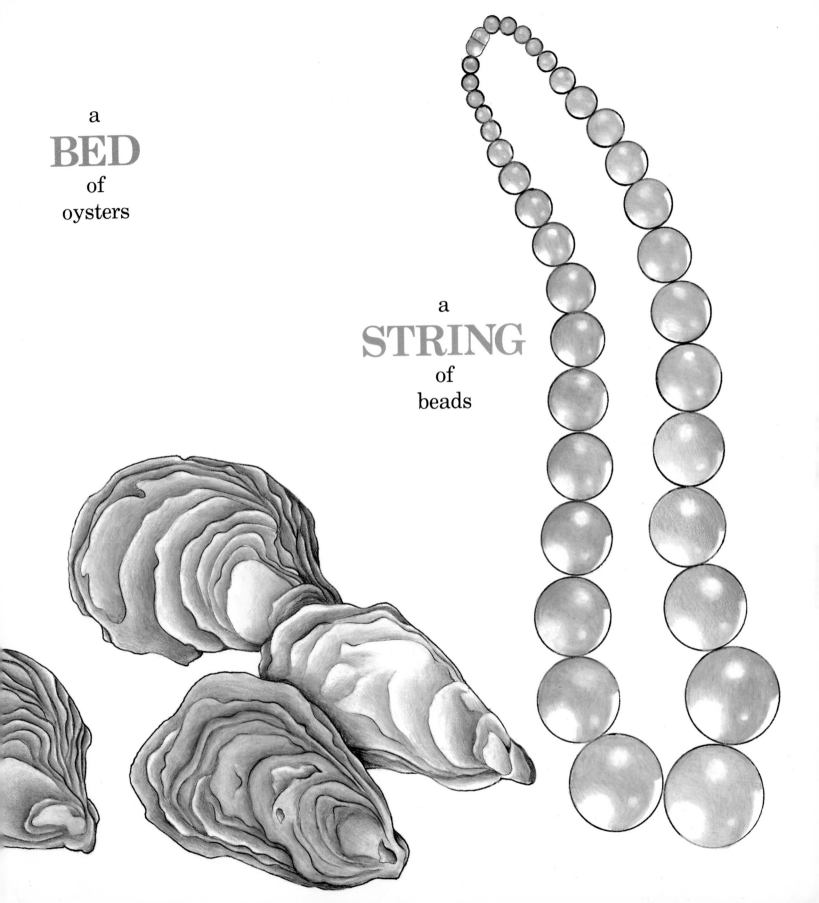

a
**BED**
of
oysters

a
**STRING**
of
beads

a
**BROOD**
of
chicks

a
CLUTCH
of
eggs

a
# LITTER
of puppies on wobbly legs

a
**PRIDE**
of lions

a
**LOCK**
of hair

an
**ARMY**
of ants
from
here to…

there....

About five hundred years ago
knights and ladies in the know
used only very special words
to describe their flocks or herds.

These words are used by us today,
but some were lost along the way,
and new ones have been added too.

I've included quite a few.

And there are more of these group terms
like **sleuth** of bears
or **clew** of worms
or **rafter** of turkeys
**walk** of snails
**leap** of leopards
**covey** of quails.

But nouns aren't all collective,
and if I'm to be effective,
I'll tell about the other nouns
and adjectives and verbs.

All of them are parts of speech.

What fun!
I'll write a book for each.

—*Ruth Heller*

<u>Note:</u> One collective noun can describe many groups, as in a **host** of angels, daffodils, monks, thoughts, or sparrows.

One group can be described by more than one collective noun as in a **gam** of whales, a **mob** of whales, a **pod** of whales, a **school** of whales, or a **run** of whales.